Better Than Gold

by Carolyn Clark
illustrated by Keith Neely

Harcourt

Orlando Boston Dallas Chicago San Diego

Visit *The Learning Site!*

www.harcourtschool.com

For many years while I was a child, my father dreamed about striking gold. We moved to California because Daddy was convinced that there was still gold to be found there.

He spent all his time down by the river, panning for gold. When he needed to make some money, he would get a job as a handyman. Daddy could build or fix anything.

We didn't need a whole lot of money. Mama grew a big garden. That's where most of our food came from. We weren't a big family. Julia and I were the only children.

In the spring of 1925, there was a lot of news about Alaska. Daddy read everything he could find. Next to looking for gold, reading was his favorite thing to do. He read that there had been a Gold Rush in 1898 around a town called Nome.

He also read about a team of sled dogs that had carried medicine through heavy snow and ice into Nome. It saved many lives.

"Jenny," Daddy said, "they say that there's so much gold in Nome, Alaska, that it washes up right on the beach."

“If there’s so much gold in Nome, Alaska,” Mama asked, “why are there so few people there?”

Daddy didn’t say a word. He turned around and gave me a sly wink.

After Julia and I went to bed, I could hear Mama and Daddy talking softly in the next room.

The next morning Daddy said, “We’re going to Alaska, at least for the summer. I promised your mama that if she doesn’t like it, we’ll come back here in the fall.”

Daddy went to the telegraph office to see about making travel plans. He came home whistling a cheery tune. “We’re all set!” he said. “We leave next week.”

The next week, we packed our things and drove to San Francisco. When we got there, Daddy sold our Model T Ford, and we boarded a ship headed for Nome, Alaska.

Ships were pretty much the only way to get people and cargo to Nome. There weren’t many roads. There weren’t any railroads or passenger airplanes, either.

Julia and I had a great time on the ship. It was mostly meant to carry cargo, so there were lots of big boxes that were good for playing hide-and-seek.

Mama gave us geography lessons. She showed us a map of where we were going. From San Francisco, we headed north on the Pacific Ocean. We passed Oregon, Washington, and some of Canada.

The farther north we went, the colder it got. It was May, but we were shivering. Finally, on the tenth day, we docked in Nome.

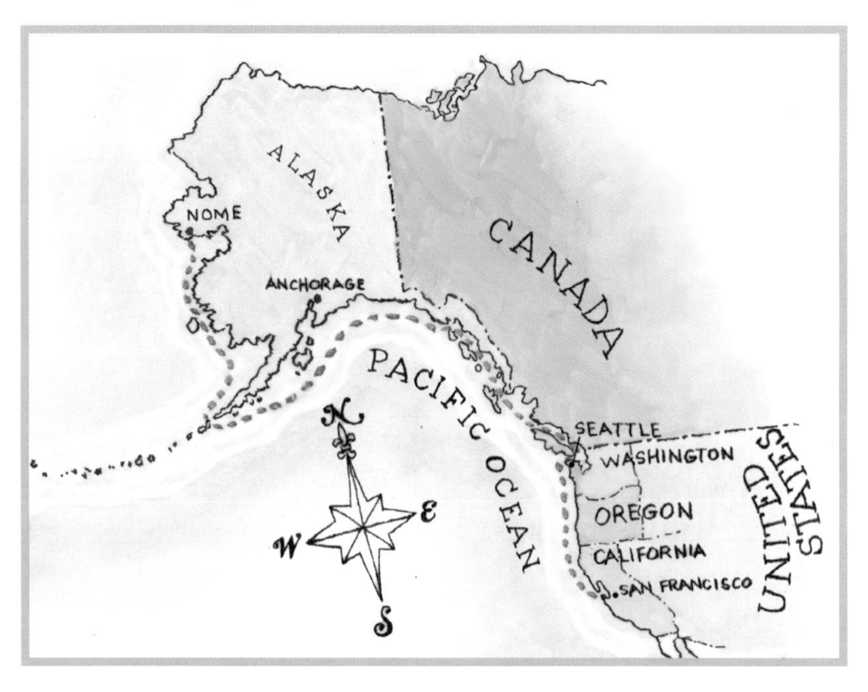

Mama and Daddy walked slowly down the gangplank, carrying our things. Julia and I skipped ahead of them.

Then I saw something interesting. A circle of people was standing with a blanket stretched between them as tightly as they could stretch it. Someone was bouncing up and down in the center of the blanket. That looked like fun!

The children who were watching were dressed differently from Julia and me. I wondered why.

Just then, a man came up to greet us. "Welcome to Nome!" he said. "I'm Louis Wolfe. What brings you here?"

"Gold," said Daddy.

"You're a little too late for gold, but you're welcome to see what you can find!"

"Excuse me, Mr. Wolfe," I said politely. "What are those people doing?"

"That's a game called 'blanket toss,'" he said. "Those children are watching their elders play. Their families have lived in Alaska for thousands of years."

"It wasn't always a game, though," Mr. Wolfe added. "Alaskan hunters would toss one hunter in the air, so he could look far and wide for game to hunt."

Mr. Wolfe turned back to Daddy. "Where are you folks staying?"

"We brought a tent. We figured we would camp out for the summer," Daddy said.

"The temperature gets pretty warm in the summer, but the ground is always frozen," Mr. Wolfe said. "Tell you what—why don't you folks come home with me?"

Mr. Wolfe guided us down the trail to his house. When we got there, he called out, "Mrs. Wolfe, we have visitors!"

A kind-looking lady came out of the house. "Why, hello! What a nice surprise!"

Mr. Wolfe said, "This is John Walters, his wife, Margaret, and their girls, Jenny and Julia. John is looking for gold. I asked them to stay with us until they find a place to settle."

"I doubt if you'll find much gold anymore, but you're welcome to stay here and try," said Mrs. Wolfe as she opened the door.

The next morning, Daddy got up early and went down to Anvil Creek to start panning for gold. Mama, Julia, and I stayed home with Mrs. Wolfe.

That became our routine. Mrs. Wolfe cooked and did laundry and mending for a lot of the men. Mama started helping her, and they became the best of friends. I had never seen Mama so happy.

Julia and I watched the children play, until one day a girl about my age asked us to come and play with them.

The girl's name was Tulugaak. She had a little sister, too, named Masak. Tulugaak showed me games, and I showed her games. Pretty soon, we were playing together every day. Before we knew it, we were best friends.

Daddy worked hard every day, looking for gold. He didn't have much luck. He found some flakes here and there, and a few tiny nuggets, just enough to keep him going.

Daddy also made friends. When he wasn't looking for gold, he was talking to the men at the Anvil City General Store.

Before long, summer was almost over. I wanted to stay in Nome. It would be awfully cold in the winter, but Tulugaak said she would show me how to stay warm.

One day, I just had to ask. "Daddy, are we going to stay here?"

Daddy stopped so he could look me straight in the eye. "I know you want to stay, Jenny, but I think we will have to go back. We don't have a place to live. We can't stay with the Wolfe family forever."

I nodded, my eyes full of tears.

The next morning, we woke up to some very strange sounds. We got dressed as fast as we could and ran outside.

It looked like the whole town was there! At least half a dozen sled dog teams were dragging sleds full of lumber.

"We heard you wanted to stay," said Mr. Wolfe. "We are going to build you a house, right next door. I'm donating the land."

Mama and Daddy were speechless, but I said, "Thank you!" and gave Mr. Wolfe a big hug.

Everyone worked all day long. The men sawed and hammered. Mama and Mrs. Wolfe cooked lunch. Tulugaak, Masak, Julia, and I carried boards and held them while the men nailed them in place. We got a few splinters, but we didn't care. We were going to stay in Nome!

Daddy told the men that he couldn't thank them enough. They said, "Oh, yes, you can! You have a real talent for fixing things, and there are a lot of things around town that need fixing. You can help us."

Winter came, and it was colder than I could have even imagined. The ground was covered with ice, and snow piled up in drifts everywhere. Luckily, we had our little house where we were warm and safe.

Daddy lost most of his interest in searching for gold after we got the house. When I asked him why, he said, “I used to think having lots of gold would make my life better. Now I know that you, Mama, Julia, and our friends here are the real treasures in life. I don’t need the other kind of gold anymore!”